Two Crazy Pigs

by Karen Berman Nagel
Illustrated by Brian Schatell

Hello Reader! — Level 2

SCHOLASTIC INC. · Cartwheel ·B·O·O·K·S· ™
New York Toronto London Auckland Sydney

We are two crazy pigs.
We lived on the
Fenster farm.

A NOTE TO PARENTS

Reading Aloud with Your Child
Research shows that reading books aloud is the single most valuable support parents can provide in helping children learn to read.
- Be a ham! The more enthusiasm you display, the more your child will enjoy the book.
- Run your finger underneath the words as you read to signal that the print carries the story.
- Leave time for examining the illustrations more closely; encourage your child to find things in the pictures.
- Invite your youngster to join in whenever there's a repeated phrase in the text.
- Link up events in the book with similar events in your child's life.
- If your child asks a question, stop and answer it. The book can be a means to learning more about your child's thoughts.

Listening to Your Child Read Aloud
The support of your attention and praise is absolutely crucial to your child's continuing efforts to learn to read.
- If your child is learning to read and asks for a word, give it immediately so that the meaning of the story is not interrupted. DO NOT ask your child to sound out the word.
- On the other hand, if your child initiates the act of sounding out, don't intervene.
- If your child is reading along and makes what is called a miscue, listen for the sense of the miscue. If the word "road" is substituted for the word "street," for instance, no meaning is lost. Don't stop the reading for a correction.
- If the miscue makes no sense (for example, "horse" for "house"), ask your child to reread the sentence because you're not sure you understand what's just been read.
- Above all else, enjoy your child's growing command of print and make sure you give lots of praise. *You are your child's first teacher—and the most important one. Praise from you is critical for further risk-taking and learning.*

—Priscilla Lynch
Ph.D., New York University
Educational Consultant

To Ian M. Nagel,
with love and thanks for all your ideas.
—K.B.N.

For Robin
—B.S.

Copyright © 1992 by Karen Nagel.
Illustrations copyright © 1992 by Brian Schatell.
All rights reserved. Published by Scholastic Inc.
CARTWHEEL BOOKS is a trademark of Scholastic Inc.
HELLO READER! is a registered trademark of Scholastic, Inc.

Library of Congress Cataloging-in-Publication Data

Nagel, Karen.
    Two crazy pigs / by Karen Nagel; illustrated by Brian Schatell.
        p.   cm. — (Hello reader)
    "Cartwheel Books."
    "Level 2 ."
    Summary: Two pigs who drive the farmer and his wife crazy with their silliness and pranks decide to move to a new farm, only to be missed by all when they leave.
    ISBN 0-590-46695-X
    [1. Pigs—Fiction.   2. Domestic animals—Fiction.]   I. Schatell, Brian, ill.   II. Title.   III. Series.
PZ7.N1345Tw   1992
[E]—dc20

                                                                91-18860
                                                                    CIP
                                                                    AC

12   11   10   9   8   7   6   5   4   3   2   2   3   4   5   6/9   23
                        Printed in the U.S.A.
            First Scholastic printing, April 1992

We tickled the hens while
they were laying eggs.

"Stop that, you crazy pigs,"
yelled Mr. Fenster.

We tied the cows' tails
together while they were
giving milk.

"Stop that, you crazy pigs," yelled Mrs. Fenster.

Instead of rolling in the mud,
we threw it at each other.

OOPS!

"Pack your bags and leave!"
yelled Mr. and Mrs. Fenster.

All the animals cried, "We'll miss you, crazy pigs!"

We went down the road to
Mr. and Mrs. Henhawk's farm.
"Do you have room here for
two crazy pigs?" we asked.

Mr. Henhawk made us a new
pigpen.

He laughed when we dipped
the sheep's tail in ink.

Mrs. Henhawk let us make
mud pies in her stove.

One day the Fensters' cow,
Shirley, came to visit.

"Will you come back to the
farm?" Shirley asked.

"The hens are not laying eggs.

The cows have stopped
giving milk."

"No," we said. "Mr. and
Mrs. Henhawk love us for
who we are — crazy pigs."

We pulled Shirley's tail and
said good-bye. Then she went
back to the Fenster farm.

One week later, all of the
Fensters' animals came to
the Henhawk farm.

Shirley spoke.
"The Fensters have moved to
the city. Do you have room
for us here?"

Mr. and Mrs. Henhawk asked
all the animals to live on
their farm.

We were very happy to have our friends back.

We rubbed everybody's faces
in mud.

We jumped on the Henhawks'
feather bed for two hours.

We were so happy! "Let's visit
the Fensters in the city for
old time's sake," we said.

"Are you kidding?" asked
Shirley.
"Are you sure?" asked
Mr. Henhawk.

"No," we said, "we're crazy!"